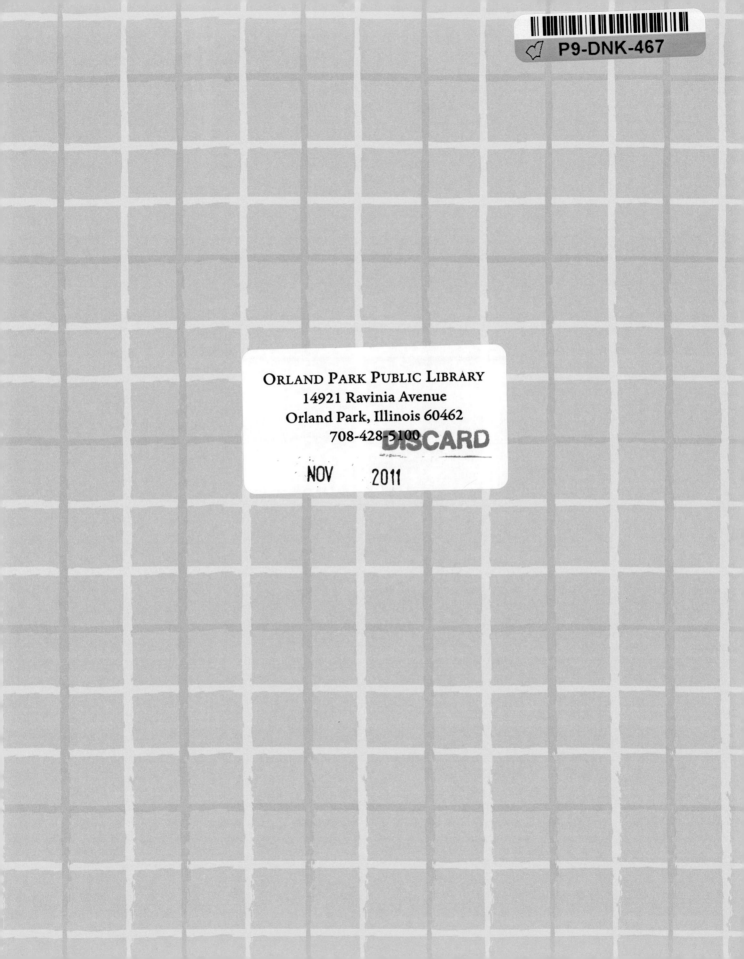

THE BELLY BOOK

For Jodi Reamer — F. M.

For Rebecca Sherman — D. Y.

A FEIWEL AND FRIENDS BOOK
An Imprint of Macmillan

THE BELLY BOOK. Text copyright © 2011 by Fran Manushkin.
Illustrations copyright © 2011 by Dan Yaccarino. All rights reserved.
Printed in July 2011 in China by South China Printing Co. Ltd., Dongguan City, Guangdong Province.
For information, address Feiwel and Friends, 175 Fifth Avenue, New York, N.Y. 10010.

Library of Congress Cataloging-in-Publication Data Available

ISBN: 978-0-312-64958-6

The artwork was created with gouache on watercolor paper.

Book design by Dan Yaccarino

Feiwel and Friends logo designed by Filomena Tuosto

First Edition: 2011

1 3 5 7 9 10 8 6 4 2

mackids.com

THE BELLY BOOK

Fran Manushkin

illustrated by

Dan Yaccarino

FEIWEL AND FRIENDS

NEW YORK

Every daughter, every son,
has their own—but only one—

with a button in the middle.
Can you guess this little riddle?

It's your belly—right in front!
Look down! You don't have to hunt.

Bellies belong to every nation.
Let's have a belly celebration!

Bellies, we love you, smooth

or hairy.

On the mountains!

On the prairie!

When our bodies need some chow,
you growl and grumble,

"Feed me NOW!"

Pizza! Pretzels! Toast and jelly!
Everything lands in you, belly.

Bellies love carrots and birthday cakes,

tofu, tacos, chocolate shakes!

Sparrow bellies cheep and chirp.

People's bellies belch and burp!

Belly buttons! Feast your eyes.
Everyone's a small surprise.
Annie has a skinny innie.
Danny has a pouty outie!

Looking closer, if you squint,
you can see a little lint.

Where it comes from, no one knows!
Here it comes—and there it goes!

Once upon a time, your mummy
grew you—right inside her tummy.

Maybe there might be another:
a baby sister? Or a brother?

Every little panda cub
loves his mama's belly rub.

**Muddy puppies need them, too—
and a rub-a-dub shampoo!**

Daddy's diving! Watch out! PLOP!

What a funny belly flop!

Itchy tummies make me wriggle.

Ticklish tummies make me giggle!

Show the world your belly dance!

Parade your bellies from here to Spain.

Bellies in the desert!

Bellies in the rain!

SPAIN

Bellies big or bellies teeny!

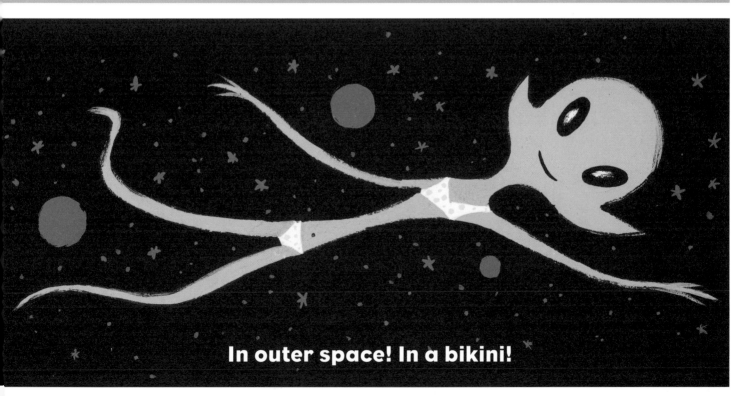

In outer space! In a bikini!

PINK BELLIES!

BROWN BELLIES!

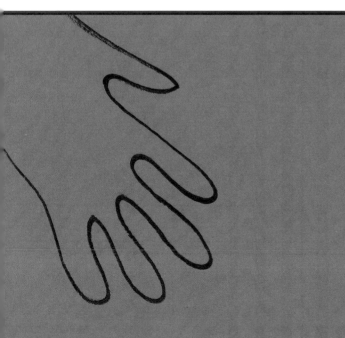

ROUND OR FLAT,

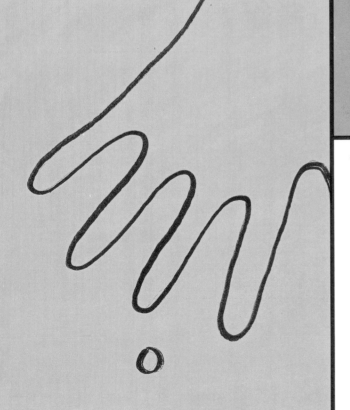

ALL DESERVE A HAPPY PAT!

Bellies, we love you!
Bellies so clever—

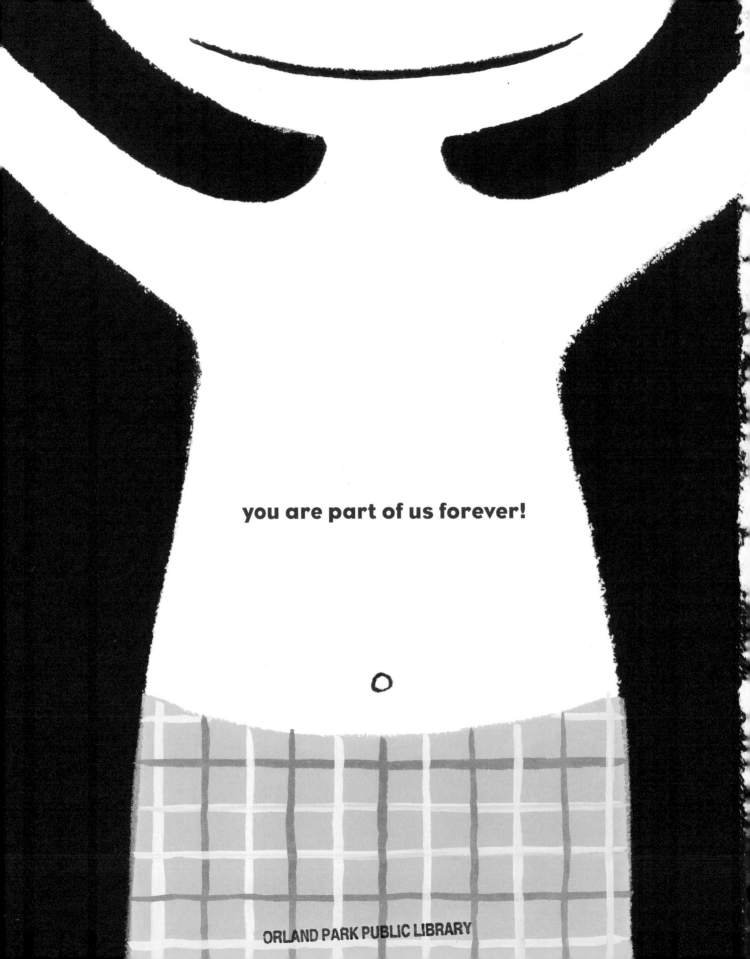

you are part of us forever!